Bartholomew's
DREAM

DEDICATION
For Tom and Jan who stand
by me through writer's
blues and pump me 'til
I'm pink again.

Bartholomew's DREAM

Patti Farmer, Illustrated by Amy Wummer

BARRON'S

All inquiries should be addressed to:
Barron's Educational Series, Inc.
250 Wireless Boulevard, Hauppauge, NY 11788

International Standard Book No.
0-8120-6403-8 (hard cover)
0-8120-1991-1 (paperback)

Library of Congress Catalog Card No. 94-9456

Library of Congress Cataloging-in-Publication Data

Farmer, Patti.
    Bartholomew's dream / by Patti Farmer ; illustrated by
Amy Wummer.
        p.   cm.
    Summary: When a young boy describes to his mother
how he rescued her when she wandered off in his dreams,
she promises to stay close by for the rest of the night.
    ISBN 0-8120-6403-8. — ISBN 0-8120-1991-1 (pbk.)
    [1. Dreams—Fiction. 2. Mothers and sons—Fiction.]
I. Wummer, Amy, ill. II. Title.
PZ7.F23815Bar   1994
[E]—dc20   94-9456
                                                    CIP
                                                    AC

PRINTED IN HONG KONG

4567   9955   987654321

It was late one night
when Bartholomew
woke up hollering,
"Mom-m-m-m!"

"I'm here, Bartholomew," said his mother.
"I had a dream!" said Bartholomew,
breathlessly. "You...me...in the jungle."
"Really?" said his mother. "Tell me."
"Try not to be scared," said Bartholomew.
"I'll try," said his mother.

Bartholomew took a deep breath.
"I dreamed you wandered off,
and when I found you, this giant
snake had wrapped itself all around you."
"Oh my," said his mother.
"Yes," said Bartholomew, "and your eyes were
bugging right out of your head."
"Oh no," said his mother.

Bartholomew nodded. "So I tore that snake away
and tied it into a pretzel."

"Thank heavens," said his mother.

"Yes," said Bartholomew.

"Then your eyes went back into your head."

"I'm glad you found me," said
Bartholomew's mother.
"But that's not all!"
"Really?" said his mother. "Tell me."
"Try not to be scared."
"I'll try," said his mother.

Bartholomew took a deep breath. "I dreamed you
wandered off, and when I found you, a huge tidal
wave had swept you into the ocean."
"Oh my," said his mother.
"Yes," said Bartholomew, "and you were
turning kind of blue."
"Oh no," said his mother.

Bartholomew nodded. "So I dragged you back to shore and pumped you till you were pink."
"Thank heavens," said his mother.
"Yes," said Bartholomew. "You don't look good in blue."

"I'm glad you found me,"
said Bartholomew's mother.
"But there's more!"
"Really?" said his mother.
"Tell me."
"Try not to be scared."
"I'll try," said his mother.

Bartholomew took a deep breath.
"I dreamed you wandered off,
and when I found you, cannibals
had stuffed you head down
in a big fiery pot."
"Oh my," said his mother.
"Yes," said Bartholomew. "and
your little feet were sticking out."
"Oh no," said his mother.

Bartholomew nodded.
"So I swung down on a vine
and yanked you out of there
as fast as I could."
"Thank heavens," said his mother.
"Yes," said Bartholomew.
"I thought you were a goner."

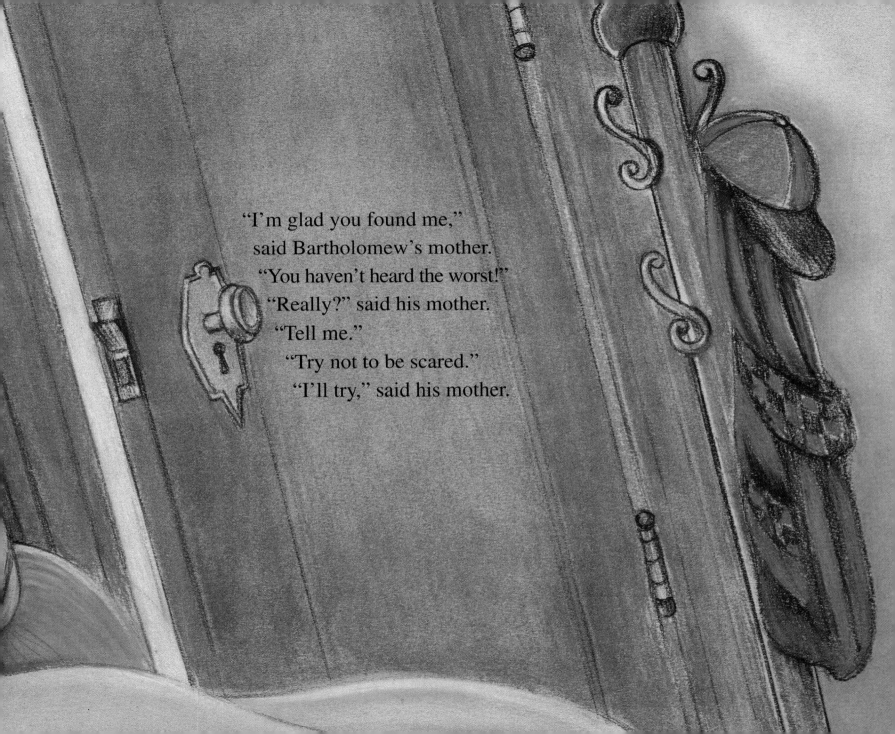

"I'm glad you found me,"
said Bartholomew's mother.
"You haven't heard the worst!"
"Really?" said his mother.
"Tell me."
"Try not to be scared."
"I'll try," said his mother.

Bartholomew took a deep breath. "I dreamed you wandered off, and you weren't with the cannibals, and you weren't with the snake, and you weren't in the ocean, and I couldn't find you anywhere."
"Oh my," said his mother.

"Yes," said Bartholomew,
"and it was getting dark."
"Oh no," said his mother.

Bartholomew nodded.
"So I closed my eyes
real tight and hollered,
'Mom-m-m-m!'

I heard you say,
'I'm here, Bartholomew.'"
"Thank heavens," said his mother.
"Yes," said Bartholomew.
"'Cause when I opened my eyes . . .

. . . you were here."
"I'm glad you found me,"
said Bartholomew's mother.
"Me too," said Bartholomew. "You're not
going to wander off anymore tonight, are you?"
"No," said his mother, hugging him gently.
                    "Good," said Bartholomew, yawning.
                            "I'm really tired."

Then he closed his eyes
and fell fast asleep.